# Dear Parent:

Congratulations! Your child is taking the first steps on an exciting journey. The destination? Independent reading!

**STEP INTO READING®** will help your child get there. The program offers five steps to reading success. Each step includes fun stories and colorful art. There are also Step into Reading Sticker Books, Step into Reading Math Readers, Step into Reading Phonics Readers, Step into Reading Write-In Readers, and Step into Reading Phonics Boxed ˹        ˺ cy program with something to interest every child

## Learning to Read, Step by Step!

**Ready to Read   Preschool–Ki**
• big type and easy words • rhyme an（
For children who know the alphabe
begin reading.

**Reading with Help   Preschoo**
• basic vocabulary • short sentences •
For children who recognize familiar
new words with help.

**Reading on Your Own   Grade**
• engaging characters • easy-to-follow
For children who are ready to read c

**Reading Paragraphs   Grades ⁚**
• challenging vocabulary • short paragr（
For newly independent readers who
with confidence.

**Ready for Chapters   Grades 2–4**
• chapters • longer paragraphs • full-color art
For children who want to take the plunge into chapter books
but still like colorful pictures.

**STEP INTO READING®** is designed to give every child a successful reading experience. The grade levels are only guides. Children can progress through the steps at their own speed, developing confidence in their reading, no matter what their grade.

Remember, a lifetime love of reading starts with a single step!

POCOYO™ © 2005–2013 Zinkia Entertainment, S.A. The POCOYO™ series, characters, and logos are trademarks of Zinkia Entertainment and are used only under license. All rights reserved. Published in the United States by Random House Children's Books, a division of Random House, Inc., 1745 Broadway, New York, NY 10019, and in Canada by Random House of Canada Limited, Toronto.

Step into Reading, Random House, and the Random House colophon are registered trademarks of Random House, Inc.

Visit us on the Web!
StepIntoReading.com
randomhouse.com/kids
www.pocoyo.com

Educators and librarians, for a variety of teaching tools, visit us at RHTeachersLibrarians.com

ISBN 978-0-449-81541-0 (trade) — ISBN 978-0-375-97167-9 (lib. bdg.)

Printed in the United States of America   10 9 8 7 6 5 4 3 2 1

STEP INTO READING®

STEP 1

# POCOYO™

# Scooter Trouble

By Christy Webster

Random House 🏠 New York

Pocoyo and Pato
take a walk.

They find
a scooter!

# It is Elly's scooter.

They will take
the scooter
to Elly.

# Uh-oh! A rock!

Pocoyo and Pato fly
into the air!

# Pato sees the scooter.

Safe landing!

# Pato is a scooter pro!

Pato the pro
wears goggles.

# Pato dodges trees.

Pato jumps!

It is time
for the big finish.

# Pato rolls down.

# Pato rolls up.

Way up!

Pato comes down.
Oh, no!

The scooter is
broken.

It was Elly's scooter!
She will not like this.

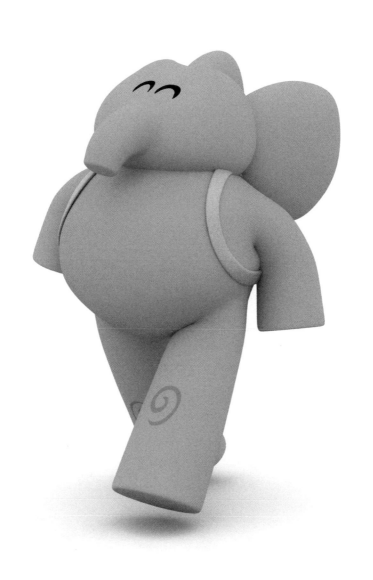

Elly is coming!

Pato pretends
to be Elly's scooter.

# Elly gets on.

# Oh, no!

Pato shows Elly
the broken
scooter.

Pato and Pocoyo
try to fix it.

They show Elly.
It breaks again!

Elly laughs.

Elly hugs.

Elly just got
a new scooter!

# Hooray for Elly!
# Hooray for friends!